The Party

and

Other Short Stories

The Party

and

Other Short Stories

FloZa

iUniverse, Inc.
Bloomington

The Party and Other Short Stories

iUniverse books may be ordered through booksellers or by contacting:

iUniverse
1663 Liberty Drive
Bloomington, IN 47403
www.iuniverse.com
1-800-Authors (1-800-288-4677)

ISBN: 978-1-4759-3720-6 (sc)
ISBN: 978-1-4759-3721-3 (ebk)

Printed in the United States of America

iUniverse rev. date: 08/10/2012

Dedicated

To my son Charles-Alexander who has brought so much love and joy to my life and hope for the future.

To my mother, brother, and sisters who sheltered us with love, continuous and abundant care and affection.

Introducing the Author

$\mathcal{F}$lorence Zohreh Zaré, FloZa, was born in Tehran in 1949 in a happy family with loving parents, one brother and two sisters.

From a very early age she enjoyed writing, as well as drawing and painting. When she was in high school she spent some time in California. Later she went to "Pahlavi University" in Shiraz and graduated in English Language and Literature.

Her first love was painting, as she has always painted since the age of ten; and her second love writing; as the events of her life have brought her to live in very different countries . . . in particular historical times.

She started her professional life as an English teacher (1972-1978), first in Tehran, Iran, with an American Company, and then in France.

Later she continued her studies in Banking and worked in an international bank for several years.

After a heart breaking separation in France in the late 1980's, she travelled to the United States together with her two-year-old son, Charles-Alexander—first to California and then to Arizona. She studied Business in North American College in Phoenix, and worked in a bank for a while . . .

She and her son travelled to Tehran in mid 1991 to stay with their family in Niavaran, a northern suburb of Tehran. The young boy could attend the French school and his mother could have an active life and support her small family.

At that time there was a French community of about one hundred people in Iran. Those years were quite challenging for Florence. As she had left Iran before the Iranian Revolution, rediscovering the country under totally different circumstances required a lot of adaptation on her part, and a permanent effort for more and more comprehension.

She continued her studies by correspondence and accomplished an MBA in Business Administration from the Pacific Western University of Los Angeles.

In Tehran she occupied a number of interesting positions in Irano-European companies, as Assistant to Managers and CEO's. Her son was also receiving a good education and overall they had a happy life, surrounded by family and friends.

Years later, when she had an opportunity to come back to France, she kept thinking about those years spent in the new Iran, a country where people spoke a language she knew well, yet everything had totally changed! The storied you read here are the result of her life experience throughout those years spent in Iran. She wrote them down so that they would settle in her mind and allow her to continue with her present life.

Her son is now an accomplished young man of 25 and the joy of her life . . .

Ever since mid 1999 she has been living near Paris, in France and working as a "Professeur d'Anglais". She has also been painting and writing . . .

The illustrations on the book cover , for "The Party", "The Happy Life of Maryam Shomali", and "I Am a Pear, I Am an Island" are original paintings by Florence Zohreh Zaré, signed, "Floza", her artist's signature.

"THE PARTY"

"The Party"

The salon formed the shape of an "L". People could come in by the far end where the entrance door was. Each time the door opened the cold winter air blew in, bringing in a lot of sunshine in its breath.

We were in sunshine country, so the bright sunny light came in through every open door, through all the windows and any pore in the wall.

There were fruit and pastries on the low tables of rectangular shape that were set up within equal distances in the middle of the passage way—a large 'L' shaped isle. There were also small plates, accompanied by little forks and spoons. The tables were neatly set and there was plenty to eat, and hot tea and coffee to drink.

A woman in black came around, carrying a large tray with little 'estekans' (especial small glasses for serving tea) and small cups of perfumed coffee. Passing by slowly, she lowered her tray in front of each guest. "Tea or coffee?" She asked now and then in the solemn way which is the manner at funeral gatherings.

When she lowered her tray for me I took an estekan of hot tea with lots of sugar and said:

"Thank you, khanoum," and started to eat some cookies.

Most of the chairs were taken. There were children running in all directions.

"Sit down and don't move around so much", said one mommy to her six or seven year old child.

Children could do most anything they wanted at any occasion in that country—one was never too harsh on them.

And if you asked people why they were so permissive with children, they would simply say:

"Well they are children and not quite grown-ups yet . . ."

My son had stayed outside to play with his cousins on the green space that was surrounded by decorative bushes.

At a later season there would be flowers everywhere. In the winter, however, you could only find flowers inside the waiting salons and not outside. These were usually white and peach-coloured gladioli. They were arranged in a number of tall crystal vases, and placed on small elegant tables here and there, creating a rather colourful scene.

—∞—

My Mom was talking with an aunt, while her silk scarf had slipped half way down her fine light brown hair. My sister was busy chatting along with the daughters of the deceased cousin. They all had eyes red from crying. It was a very sad occasion and nobody was happy so to speak.

—∞—

I was sitting on the far end of the 'L'-shaped salon, facing the light. For a moment it seemed to me that my father was also sitting there in front of me, a little further to the left, with his back to the light. He was wearing a white outfit, something like judo clothes. He had no shoes on. He did not look sad, just patient and there was a glitter in his eyes. Was it a tear?

He was as he used to be during his lifetime. His eyes had the colour of honey and were very attractive . . . His hands were laying calmly on his knees! How could this be? We had lost him ten years before—also on a cold winter's day—but I could feel his presence, and see him there, I was sure, for a while . . .

The cousin that we had just lost was one of his favourite nephews, a doctor in his late forties, a very young age to die indeed . . . He had left behind a young widow and three daughters.

He had been a very kind and tolerant man. Before his illness he had managed the medical services of an entire province in the northern part of the country for many years. We all regretted him immensely.

—๗—

Another young woman passed through the row of tables and offered us some dates on a large plate. These were not just any dates—a special prayer had been said and blown onto them, so they had a sacred character. They were decorated with coconut powder. You had to take one with a lot of care and eat it while praying for the deceased and his family. They were known to possess special beneficial powers on the living—as well as the soul of the deceased.

Had it not been for the sunshine that filled up the room, despite the early morning hour, it would have been a really sad sight.

—๗—

It was about 9 O'clock when *She* came in. A very tall and beautiful woman all dressed in black. Everyone else was also wearing black, but that colour, seemed to have a particular significance on her. She had an indescribably perfect and serene profile, and very pale skin. You could tell by the rounded shape of her elegant black scarf that she was wearing her jet-black hair up.

She opened the door decidedly with one hand, and stepped in, while holding the strangest handbag in the other!!! It was a medium sized, shiny black handbag with a rounded shape on top and decorated with two similarly round flowers. She was holding it with her right hand, in a businesslike manner, as if it was meant for something of utmost importance . . . something as important as . . . my cousin's life!

"*She* must be *Death*", I thought. "She has come to carry away my cousin's soul in her bag!"

She took a few steps and sat down facing the light. She held her head slightly bent and you could see her black eyes looking calmly at the door as if she was expecting someone to come in. There was a shadow of a smile on her full lips. She looked neither sad nor happy, but sort of . . . *contained*, as she sat there holding her strange handbag on her knees.

Despite the constant humming of the voices I could hear the silence that surrounded her.

It is difficult to describe just how I felt, a cool air current passed in front of me . . . I stopped eating. My mouth remained open, with the cookie in my hand.

I sat straight and started looking around me. My cousin for whom the ceremony was being held was sitting a few seats away to my right. I looked again with surprise, but he was gone!

I could swear I had seen him sitting there calmly in grey flannel trousers and the same colour polo shirt with long sleeves and the neck buttons open. He also had a black belt and black shoes. Yes, he was wearing shoes, the kind that have straps on them. He had put his left foot forward and his hands were joined together on his lap. I think he was even trying to say something . . . but his lips moved without making a sound.

—〰—

My son ran in through the door, making his way towards me through the people and tables.

"Mommy, Mommy, could you peel an orange for me?" He said, still breathless from his game.

I held him close to me warming up his cold red cheeks.

"No, Darling it's time to go outside and follow the procession."

Other children came in from their games to find their parents. There was going to be a big crowd moving and they had to stay close to their Moms and Dads.

Most people were standing now, women gathering their handbags, gloves and shawls, covering the children up. Men were moving slowly towards the door.

I looked around *She* was gone—*She was nowhere to be seen*. Had she already left the 'religious ceremony' with my cousin's soul? It was quite a mystery!

I joined my sister and the three mournful young girls, as I was holding my son's hand tight and making sure he had his warm bonnet on. My brother and his wife were already outside, walking slowly towards the 'Hammam' were the corps was being prepared.

We were now all moving towards the door, leaving the vast "L" shaped Waiting-Reception Room to the half empty tea glasses, to the knives and forks lying disorderly on small porcelain plates, to the half eaten apples and peeled oranges, to the colourful fruit and pastry on large decorative plates, to the remaining prayer-dates, and the tall branches of multi-coloured flowers, red, white and peach gladioli in transparent vases, that were set here and there on small elegant tables . . .

—ᴟᴟ—

A few weeks later in a family party I saw that beautiful young woman again. This time she was smiling and talking to everyone! She was wearing a red dress and her hair looked much lighter. She was almost blond! What a lovely smile. She was a new bride, married to one of my far distant cousins. We cannot know everyone; we have such a large family. I had a deep feeling of relief . . . *So* She wasn't "*Death* personified" after all, coming to carry somebody's life away . . .

Florence Zohreh Zaré (FloZa), November 2006

The Jewel Village
(Javaherdeh)

*T*he car was hooting along the road that whirled up the mountain. The forest was on both sides of the road, green woods where no one seemed to have trespassed in a long time. This part of the road to the Jewel Village was very shady. A mysterious fog was clinging to the trees, to the car, and all the way down to the grey asphalted road, as it unrolled in front of us. It felt like passing through white cotton. If we reached out our hands we could hold some of it and bring it into the car!

"This is not the fog, you realise of course", my brother said, as he held out his left arm into the cloud, continuing to drive with his right hand, "we're driving through the clouds . . ."

No we had no idea, but it was lovely passing through the clouds in the cool early morning air.

—⁂—

We had left Mr. Ali's house very early to avoid the heat of the day. It could become unbearable in the car despite the air-conditioning. His house was situated near the sea. He lived on the third floor with his wife and two young children. They rented the first two floors, which formed a duplex, to tourists during the weekends and the summer holidays.

My brother had become quite good friends with him. All we needed to do was to give him a call from Tehran, before setting off for our weekend, and he would hold his apartment for us.

He was a very pleasant fellow with an unworried smiling face, as most of the people living on the shores of the Caspian Sea.

He also held a small super market with his wife a little further down on the same boulevard. There was a small garden with plants and flowers. At night, as the boulevard outside was very dark and deserted, he would let us bring in our car,

Going to the hotel would not be as much fun. There would be constraints. We wouldn't be allowed to go into each other's rooms. The rules would forbid it; we would have to wear the scarf for the meals; we wouldn't be able to do this; and we wouldn't be able to do that. Only children could have lots of fun in a hotel.

Some evenings, though, we went to the Great Ramssar Hotel—in memory of the good old days—to have ice cream in the huge panoramic lounge, or on the terrace viewing the entire city. Meanwhile children could play computer games in the game-rooms. And sometimes there would be a good film showing at the movie theatre of the hotel.

Other than that we were much happier at Mr. Ali's private house where we could do whatever we wanted. We bought everything we needed form his small, but clean and modern super market.

There was not a worry. The sea was within walking distance, about half a mile of warm silver sand away.

—⫯—

The people from the North of the Alborz Mountains have a particular kindness. A remarkable availability is normally attributed to them. Counting from the Old Persian times to the present, the country has been a battlefield to many wars. The people from the North, the 'Shomali', however, have hardly ever been conquered by any 'enemy'. They have always been protected by the high Alborz Mountains that stand tall and strong between the provinces of Gilan, Mazandaran and Golestan on the shores of the Caspian Sea, and the rest of the country. The population is extremely kind and easy to live with. They can always be counted on for their 'good service with a smile', hospitality and friendliness.

—⫯—

That morning, as any other morning when we wanted to go shopping down town Ramssar, we took the boulevard, turned right at the cross roads and drove along a second large and fabulous boulevard, with two rows of trees on each side. All along the boulevard there were spacious and comfortable-looking houses, painted white and pink. The gardens were normally vast, and filled with trees, particularly orange trees. Flowers were also plentiful and their fragrance would follow you everywhere in the air.

As we approached the mountains, we had to turn left and pass by the Bazaar Quarter where the major shops and stores were gathered—all in a handful of streets. At that early hour only bakeries were open. Some people were standing in line waiting for fresh bread to come out of the oven . . . 'Nan-e-Sangak', 'Nan-e-Lavash', and 'Nan-e-Barbary', each one more appetizing and delicious than the other.

This was also the quarter of the Main Mosque. Here and there some religious people were crossing the street in their traditional outfits, the 'Turban' and the 'Aba'. That weekend was actually a religious holiday, as there are so many others during the year. Even the religion, with its harsh and unbending rules seemed to have softened in the sunny, damp and dreamy air of the Caspian Sea, filled with odorous plants and flowers. Here one hardly felt the imposing weight of the religious law as one permanently would in some other parts of the country.

We had to go around the big mosque and cross an old stone bridge in order to take the road to the Jewel Village, and so we did. Soon we left behind the green fields along the river, approached the immense mountains, got closer and closer, and drove into the woods. The road was climbing the mountain and it was quite perceptible that we were gaining altitude.

—◊◊◊—

Half way to the top of the mountain at the turn of the cool and shady road there appeared a small green hill with a few round tables and some chairs. A little further away on a wooden bench, covered by a colourful rug, three men were smoking the water-pipe, 'nargilé'. There was a small one-story cottage with wide open windows. We could also see a band of chickens running on the grass in every direction. A young waiter was bringing tea on a tray to the men on the bench.

"Here's a nice place to stop and have some tea", said my sister-in-law. "As we left very early I didn't bring anything to drink".

Everyone agreed. So we parked the long navy blue car by the side of the road and walked to the small hill on the turn of the road. It felt very chilly even as we were cuddling around the round table. White clouds were surrounding the little green hill and the sun could only shine through them timidly.

A young man, wearing large village trousers and a hand-knit jumper on a white shirt came to us with his tray and said that it was good that we had stopped there, as there were no other 'cafes' before Javaherdeh on the top of the mountain. We were happy to hear that and asked for hot tea and cheese and bread for everyone.

—∿—

One more hour of driving and we reached the top. It was a spectacular sight. The sun was shining brightly on the mountain top and the clouds were now below us! The mountain was standing out of the clouds and we could finally see the Jewel Village. It was sheltered by trees and huge yellow rocks partly covered by vegetation.

Another curve of the road and we were there. It was like no other place. It resembled no other village that I had seen before. It felt like floating in another time and space, or rather it felt as if time had been left behind somewhere along the way. The road curled around a terribly tall and imposing cliff and entered the village.

Small stone houses of light colour clung there to the rocks, leaning on the mountain with steep front gardens. Trees had sprung from the rocks and special high-altitude flowers, coloured the landscape in shades of yellow and blue. It was quite a sight. The street turned and mounted into the village.

Then we reached a very large square.

"This must be the village centre", I thought.

There was an immense and strong tree facing us on the other side of the square. The square was empty. Only large pieces of light grey stone, the kind that is found in the Iranian mountains, covered the soil. A quiet village square covered by large pieces of stone.

On one side of the square I noticed a black "shape" moving. We had to drive around this square to attain the other streets of the village. As we pulled nearer and nearer, a woman could be distinguished. She was bending on a large piece of flat stone, holding a tall white candle in one hand.

As we drew nearer we could see her pale face and fine features. She looked like Ludmila Tcherina the famous ballet dancer. She had such graceful movements. She also reminded me of Dorna . . . , one of my English professors at Shiraz University, a beautiful English woman . . .

We were very near now and I could see teardrops shining on her cheeks.

It was quite out of this world, this lonely woman in the middle of the vast, empty square, on the top of a mountain, leaning on what looked like a tomb, holding her tall white candle and shedding tears of sorrow in silence . . .

I thought to myself, as tears rolled down *my* cheeks:

"If I had lost someone desperately, hopelessly and unforgivingly dear to me, this is where I would morn him . . ."

—ᖚ—

We spent the afternoon with the village people sitting on the cliffs on the right hand side of the mountain, the sunny side. It was their Heaven-made park. Hundreds of cliffs formed the side of the mountain. There were natural paths among the cliffs where one could pass easily. A particular type of vegetation had grown here and there. The cliffs were warmed by the heat of the sun. We were told that it was the favorite Friday-afternoon-activity of the village people to come here, meet one another and sit around on the cliffs and chat. Young people would find their friends, and families would have picnics. A few young men were selling barbequed corn and, 'clouches' special biscuits from the region. Our children were happy to have some. It was a real treat.

Never had a group of people seemed happier and more peaceful to me than these isolated villagers getting tanned, leaning against *their cliffs* by the side of *their mountain*. They looked as if they wanted to be nowhere else in the world. They seemed to be ever enjoying their calm life in the warmth of their Heavenly Sun.

—ᖚ—

As we felt the cool hand of the evening reaching out for the mountain we set off down the winding road towards the city. A dip into the clouds and we found ourselves back in the woods. The fresh evening air was replacing the warmth of the afternoon. The radio was playing religious songs . . . My brother put on a music cassette. It was Mozart.

As we got further away from Jewel Village it got darker and darker. Around seven o'clock we arrived at our mid-way café. Our children were hungry and couldn't wait all the way to Ramssar, so we stopped to have supper.

The young waiter and his family were glad to see us again. This time he invited us to sit on the benches covered with rugs. Then he said:

"The chickens are sleeping". "Come and have a look if you want."

We followed him to the other side of the house and there they were, on a small, covered balcony. Indeed the chickens were sound sleep.

"Go ahead choose one and I will make you very good Kebab rapidly."

The idea astonished us there and then and we said:

"Oh no, please don't wake them up (they were sleeping so peacefully), we can eat something else!"

So he left and brought us some homemade bread with cheese and fruit.

It was a very good and healthy supper. Our children had climbed the rocks all afternoon and had a hard time staying awake. The young man lit some candles and put them on the metal garden table for us. We sat there, cuddled against one another biting into the hot village bread that was filled with fresh cheese, and swallowed all with gulps of perfumed tea specially made for us. The meal had been made with such good intentions that it was a real pleasure to eat . . .

—⁊⁊—

The night was dark and blue as we set off down the road. My son was sleeping with his blond head on my shoulder. My brother's sons were also sleeping. I couldn't help thinking about the delicate woman with the white candle and what had caused her such deep sorrow. It was a long while before we could see the city lights . . .

Florence Zohreh Zaré (FloZa) April 2006

The Dream

F irst thing I remember, we were in a car with all the family members. There was a road we had to drive down . . . How steep it was! We rode down and down and it seemed endless. Finally we made it downhill and reached a lake . . . apparently a nice one. There were some people walking in different directions by the side of the lake, looking for something. Something had to be found and everyone felt concerned . . . There seemed to be a contest . . . or a lottery, a prize-draw, something very important that the radio kept on announcing. No matter where we were, we could hear the announcements coming from the loud speakers . . .

Next thing I knew . . . I was climbing up some sandy yellow hills around the lake. We were going up this time, but the lake was still close by, within reach. There was no sign of the large black car that had driven us down the hill . . . nor was there any sign of the family members. They had all, vanished, and disappeared! There was just me and my little sister . . .

———

I was climbing the yellow hills with my sister . . . who had suddenly become very young. It looked as if she were six or seven years old. The air was very hot and at times we felt like taking a dip in the lake. The water, though, seemed to be too warm! Quite warm vapors were rising from the surface of the lake constantly, filing up the air, and making it difficult to breath . . .

———

Suddenly we saw a beautiful baby there, lain cautiously in the folds of the yellow hill. He was securely placed so he would not fall.

"What a gorgeous baby", I thought, "we must find his parents", and I picked him up.

Holding him carefully in my arms, as babies can be fragile, I noticed that he was just wearing a diaper, white shorts and a small white top. He was a very fine baby with chubby arms and legs, and full, rosy cheeks. His hair was wavy, and very nice hair he had! He waved his arms . . . and smiled at me cheerfully . . .

How did I know it was a baby boy? Well I don't know, I just knew that. There was a nice determined look in his eyes. I did not know which color they were. Maybe they were deep blue.

So here we were, my sister and I, carrying the baby and climbing the hills to the top to reach the city.

"We must find his parents", I said.

Then the baby talked to me!

"*I* am the prize of the lottery", he said in a very natural manner, as if it was normal for babies to talk!

He was the amir of the country in which we were lost and he was taking part in the "National Game".

I started to think: "what a strange country and what strange people. They put their baby amir out there on the yellow hills by the side of a steaming lake, for the winner to find"! He seemed to be thoroughly enjoying the game though, so I stopped thinking those thoughts . . .

Suddenly I was overwhelmed by an immense feeling of joy. "I must have won the prize"

Then naturally I started to wonder: "What's the idea, what's the deal?" . . . and continued walking with the baby in my arms . . . He mumbled something in my ear. He was being very discrete about it, and tried to keep the mystery of the game.

"You must read this", said he, looking at the small note that had been squeezed into a little medallion and attached to his shirt with a tiny safety pin.

For some reason I felt confident, filled with anguish but confident, and did not feel any urgency to do so. Then I replied hurriedly: "I'll read that later" . . . , we must find a way out of this place first, we have to go up the hill, and find our way to the city center".

—∿—

He did not insist and kept on smiling. I looked around; my sister was further away on the hill. She was wearing a nice little white dress with designs of small red flowers. Looking for seashells on the sand, she was being very carefree only as little girls can be . . .

I was filled with enthusiasm and emotion now . . . where to go, what to do? "I have to go to town and collect my prize . . ."

I took a moment and looked around only to realize that my sister had disappeared from the scenery! It was as if a magic wind had carried her away on a magic carpet. There only remained me, and the beautiful, healthy-looking baby . . .

—◦◦—

As pages turn in a dream without transition, we then found ourselves in a small street not far from the lake, facing a little square. There was an inn on the opposite side . . . or was it a café? . . . I crossed the street and pushed the door open, holding the baby in my arms.

Inside the inn there was not much light, but the air was cool. There were a number of tall stools by the counter. Some customers were hanging around here and there with a lot of space between them!!! They all seemed to be floating around with an air of indifference . . . The bartender answered my questions as he was drying some glasses with a kitchen cloth.

Somehow I knew we were in a European country. "It can't be Greece . . ." I was thinking, "Perhaps we're in Holland . . ."

No, the bartender did not know how I could go up the extremely steep street and reach the Capital above. There was no public transport . . . There were no buses . . . no taxies.

—◦◦—

There was no time to lose. Nobody seemed to be paying any particular attention to us, so we left that cool and dark inn.

Outside in the street, where the sun was shining brightly, there was a small side-garden.

A group of men were standing around an old black car, resembling London taxies. They were wearing black suits. One of them was also wearing a black hat! They had dark mustaches, and were hanging around there, in the shade of the trees, with no special purpose, or so it seemed . . . There was a resemblance between these fellows and the "Professor Tournnesoles" from the comic stories, "Tin Tin". They were all looking at me motionlessly.

I asked them whether they could drive me uptown. They responded that they couldn't, but that they could keep the baby for me while I was looking for a way out of those earthly depths. Although we had good sunshine and I had no tangible reason to doubt of their good will, I said "No, thank you", and I moved on.

—ᴍ—

The baby was now wearing a pair of dark framed glasses now. That made him look a little serious despite his kind eyes and the continual smile on his face. Why was he taking part in this game? Maybe this was a way for him to observe the population of his town and get to know his subjects better. After all he was the amir of the country! He could judge as he liked.

There was no time for such thoughts and reflections so I moved on.

—ᴍ—

Next thing I remember, I was traversing a long, wide and dark corridor in a particular woman's house with the baby in my arms. Right there in front of us, the woman was flying the two sides of a huge brown door wide open in a theatrical manner. Her dress was a long white medieval gown, with very long sleeves. They flew around in the air as she opened her arms high and wide.

Once the huge brown door was open, I could see a very high ceiling and white walls. They looked very white indeed under the bright light that poured in through a row of high windows. At the same time it was a very colorful sight, because of all the triangular flags that were hanging from the walls; green, orange, red and yellow flags.

The room was very brightly lit as compared to the long and dark corridor behind us. The baby was still in my arms, looking restless and impatient.

This woman with her long white robe and long dark hair was making nervous gestures, looking as if she had just stepped out of a Greek tragedy . . . or some medieval household. She shook her head from one side to the other, and waved her arms around in the long white sleeves. She had no patience at all to explain things to me. She only made me understand that there were no means of transport uptown. I was getting tired of this mystery and yet I wasn't ready to give up!

There I was, holding the wonderful baby, who was now looking quite serious, and not amused any more . . .

—⚬—

Then I heard the ringing of the telephone . . . and surprised . . .

I woke up! It took me a while to realise that it was just a dream! Yet how real it seemed, as some dreams do.

How involved we get to feel about the stories that we live in our dreams. I was sitting there in my bed, damp with transpiration, and wondering what happened to the wonderful baby. The very first thought that crossed my mind was:

"Why didn't I look to see what the message said?" . . . "now I'll never know . . ." "Why didn't I ask the baby himself what to do . . . where to go . . . who to see?" . . . "He seemed to be quite communicative and very knowledgeable indeed . . . If I had only listened to him" . . . "Why was I so sure of myself, why did I think I knew better?" "Now I'll never know what the message said . . . , Oh how frustrating, what anguish!"

Florence Zohreh Zaré (FloZa), August 2004

THE HAPPY LIFE OF
MARYAM SHOMALI

The Happy Life of Maryam Shomali

*S*aturdays are the cleaning lady's days. That is when she comes to clean my Mom's apartment. Some years ago we had Miss Sakina. She was great, a lovely and very good natured woman. She also used to come on Saturdays.

At that time I lived at my Mom's in Tehran. That was when my son, Charles-Alexander, attended the French-International School in the city. It was quite a blessing that we had the cleaning ladies, because I had to work on Saturdays and there was no school. Friday and Saturday formed the school weekend. Saturday was the first day of the week for working people. So it was impossible to skip it.

Indeed the week starts on Saturday and ends on Friday in Iran. Foreign Embassies and Institutions though, make Friday and Saturday their weekend—some kind of reconciliating arrangement between the Christian Calendar and the Persian Calendar.

As my Mom lived in the United States during more than half the year at that time, there would be no one at home on Saturdays and my son would be all by himself. Naturally it is not recommended to leave a six-seven-year-old child alone at home. With Miss Sakina (Sakina Khanoum) coming on Saturdays this problem was resolved. I did not need to hire an extra baby-sitter. She was very kind and patient with children and my son, Charley, really liked her. The reason being that she approved of everything he did with good humor; cooked his favorite dishes; and looked after him and the friends he invited to study and play with, on Saturdays.

Charley and I had made a deal together, that he could invite only *one* of his friends each Saturday. He always managed, however, to invite two or three, and got away with it without much trouble. This was due to Sakina

Khanoum's lovely and understanding character. Anyhow, in Iran we are very permissive and kind with children. They pretty much get all that they desire and wish for. That is probably the reason why my son has kept such good memories of his childhood years.

Coming back to our Saturdays with Sakina Khanoum, I would be at work and would not worry about a thing, because everyone always got along so well, thanks to Sakina's tactful management of the group of kids. I would come back from work to find my son, his friends and our cheerful blond housekeeper, with her all too kind and generous smile.

—⁂—

So those were the days of Sakina Khanoum. For the toasted part of the story, she has many children (I say *has* because she's still around . . .), they are nice looking young men and women now. She has rented her house, situated in the southern quarters of the city, and has rented a large apartment further to the north, in order to be closer to the families for whom she works. She shares her lodging with three of her children who are working and bringing in some income. Furthermore, she works less and less now, and has limited her families to only three. That is the family with whom she lived as an adolescent and grew up together with her younger brother (he continues to be their gardener and guardian), a second family, and my sister's family.

We still see her quite regularly, and go to parties where she has prepared the table. Lovely tables too she prepares. She is an excellent cook and we all enjoy her talents very much. She told me once that she had learnt good cooking from her deceased husband who had been one of the well-appreciated cooks at the Royal Court.

Yes, her life story is quite touching. She was very much in love with her husband who was a very kind and considerate man. They had eight children together as proof of their love and affection.

Everyone appreciates her very much and the families she works for are always very kind to her, as well as to her children. They always furnish her with everything that she needs. This goes from clothes she may need to attend a party, the funds she may need to have lovely wedding celebrations for her daughters, or doctors' fees, medical expenses, and so on.

—⁂—

Actually, this is the way that housekeepers and people working for families live in Iran. Quite often families who appreciate their work take into account all their needs. And this is a permanent rule. Each group helps them in such a way that the needs of all their family members are satisfied. It resembles a combination of small 'Social Security Systems'. You never neglect a person in need, especially when they work for you. It is not paternalism; it is a kind of charity system and tradition that works rather well.

People can be very charitable. This state of being permanently charitable is very much encouraged by the Islamic Religion, and it is practiced very naturally. They need something, they mention it nicely, and it is offered to them if possible. It is usually a win-win situation. The requests are normally within reasonable limits. So everyone feels comfortable with this system. (How else would people of modest origins make a decent living, I wonder?)

—※—

Before the Revolution the helping people would eat in the kitchen. Nowadays, however, since most people have moved into apartments, they usually have lunch around the dining room table, together with the lady of the house and the children . . . at least in our family they do.

—※—

So that was about Sakina Khanoum. Our children call her "Sisi" affectionately. We still see her quite often at my sister's, and we follow up the lives of her children, the careers of her sons-in-laws, births of her grandchildren and so on and so forth.

—※—

Now, dealing with Maryam khanoum is another pair of sleeves.

The one thing you remember about her is her smile. Her eyes also smile. She is pretty tall and athletically built—perhaps originally she was meant to be a swimming champion or something . . . She has pale skin and dark hair that she wears up most of the time, in something like a pony tail. She always wears a pair of long, dangling gold earrings that match her gold necklace and bracelets.

It is not easy to offer Maryam clothes, because she is taller than most of us, the women in the family, that is. She usually wears a long and narrow skirt, navy blue with designs of big white roses . . . together with a white sweater or a T-shirt with a nice round "décolleté" over her big breasts. Physically she is nice and energetic. Despite her long skirt she is very active, runs around quickly and gets things done in no time at all—and she always smiles.

We can offer clothes and shoes to her twin sons, Ali and Hamid. They are nice looking young men, around seventeen by now. Since they look really very much alike you can never tell one form the other. They both have a big smile and a funny, loud laughter—Maybe Hamid laughs a little bit more than Ali.

As children they used to come to the house often, and play football with our children. We had a small 'football field' in the garden with goals and everything, also a ping-pong table under the pillars, some bicycles, and skateboards and so on. It was a truly ideal playground for children and their friends.

Speaking of Maryam's twins. One of them studies better than the other. The one who is not very keen on studying has taken up apprenticeship to become a mechanic. I don't know what the other one is doing. They are both pretty pleasant fellows, and of course their mother's major concern.

The third or the first important person in Maryam's life is her husband Gholam-Ali, or as my younger sister calls him, 'Michael'.

He is a butcher and works for a very large and famous butcher shop in the north of the city. Whenever he comes to visit, he brings the family some very good and selected meat!

He is very tall and well built. He has green eyes and light brown hair; he wears a beard, and has a kind and shy smile.

Whatever you say to him he smiles. In fact I think the secret of this family is their spontaneous and good natured smile.

They are from the north of Iran, the part of the country that we all call 'Shomal'. For a while they lived in the house with our family in a large studio which is a sort of a guest house for visiting friends, and family members. Later on they bought an apartment in Karadj—a suburban town to the west of Tehran.

We have been there to witness their happiness, evolution and development. Their life story could be subject of an interesting novel. The title could be: "Come With The Revolution", rhyming with: "Gone With the Wind" . . . But they don't talk to you about the Revolution all the time, they just live their lives.

Indeed, Maryam's life story is very touching and admirable, for she has succeeded in having everything a woman of her status could wish for. How did she do that? Well, with the help of her exceptional common sense and force of character. But let's hear it in her own words . . .

—∞—

It was the first or second day after my arrival in Tehran. I was just waking up in the dry morning air. We leave the air-conditioning on, even during the night, to have cool air and humidity. It can get so hot and dry during the summer!

—∞—

In my Mom's home I sleep on the floor. There are two large bedrooms. Her own bedroom and the one she has for her guests. When I visit with my son, he sleeps on the bed, and I on a large mattress on the floor. Although now that he is a tall teen-ager, he sleeps on the mattress on the floor, and I on the bed.

There is a beautiful plant in this room. It is nearly a tree, with very fine leaves. There is an antique dressing table with lots of drawers and a tall mirror. There are also some nicely framed pictures of our children—my son, my nieces and nephews—showing them at different ages, as well as a portrait that I had painted of my Mom when I was a teen-ager. It's a lovely portrait. There she is smiling in her golden frame above the telephone table. The bed is made of the same kind of wood as the dressing table, and it is decorated with fine golden designs. The carpet is in the tones of red.

The carpet in her own bedroom has turquoise and light beige designs (her favorite colors). In her room she has kept another one of my paintings. A beautiful Indian woman in a lovely sari sitting in a garden. Obviously a maharaja's wife. She likes my paintings and has hung them all over her apartment. She is the most devoted and reliable fan of my artwork.

There are two in the haul that goes from the bedrooms to the dining room. There is a portrait of a young woman reading a book, and one of a small boy playing in the garden. There is large painting of red and orange flowers in the dining room, and in her living room there are two landscapes of mountains and villages of the north of Iran. There is also another painting there showing two cottages by a lake, composed by an unknown artist. My Dad had bought this during one of his trips and my Mom is particularly fond of it.

As you enter the dining room, you can admire your own portrait, your entire bust, in an oval silver frame, decorated with silver flowers. She has always kept her wedding mirror there, above a small oak wood buffet. We always sit around her dining room table. The space is very bright and inviting. In the center there is a very fine table made of oak wood, and eight chairs. The chairs are of the same wood and have mustard color seats. The backs have rounded shapes and designs. The two chairs for the two extremities have arms in the same shapes.

On the other side of the white columns is the living room. Her large coach and armchairs are also of the color mustard. There are many multicolor, handmade cushions on the sofa and the carpets are fine and multicolor as well.

My Mom has a good friend who is a carpet specialist. She goes to the villages herself and selects the designs. We always buy carpets from her collections. She collects things you don't find in shops or galleries.

So in her living room and dining room, separated by white columns, and surrounded by a multitude of windows and curtains of white lace, not to forget the lovely plants, we see colours that remind us of Kerman, Naiin, Kashan and even Russia . . . , Iran's large northern neighboring country.

—∞—

In the morning people come and have breakfast with my Mom. The breakfast table is set as early as seven o'clock. My Mom is an early riser. She likes to have breakfast and watch the morning news. Then she likes to read poetry. There is tea in special transparent tea glasses, 'Lighvan' cheese, homemade jam, and fresh bread from the bakery 'Nan-e-Lavash, and Nan-e-Barbary', delicious kinds of bread that you can also put in the toaster. Maryam usually sets the breakfast table when she arrives.

There is always someone to help—The children also help—when they are around—set the table, clear the table and do some of these activities . . .

—m—

So I woke up to the sound of people talking in the dining room. We always leave all the doors open. I went to the bathroom, my Mom's lovely green and yellow bathroom, to put some water on my face and brush my hair.

Maryam was sitting at the dining room table with my Mom and they were talking. As she saw me arrive, she got up with joy and came to me with open arms and a happy smile:

"Welcome home Zohreh khanoum, it's so good to see you after so many months", she said as she held me in her arms. She has a good, warm embrace . . .

"It's good to see you too", I replied, smiling back.

I kissed my Mom Good Morning and pulled out a chair and sat down.

"How's everything? How's the family?"

"Oh good, good, everyone is doing well", "I'll bring you some tea".

She went into the kitchen and came back with a glass of newly prepared, honey colored tea, and gently put it next to my breakfast plate. I thanked her, and she continued:

"Gholamali is working this summer as usual, Hamid is in summer school and Ali has started to work with a mechanic as an apprentice, thank God." "I always ask Maman Simin about you."

—m—

Everyone calls my Mom, Maman Simin as her name is Simindokht— meaning daughter of silver. She had an older sister who went to Heaven at the early age of 54 and her name was Irandokht—daughter of Iran. There are some names like that in the Iranian history—Pourandokht and Azarmidokht—They were daughters of a king in ancient Persian history. The girls' names I like the most are Roxanna and Annahita . . .

So, we sat down and had breakfast. The bread was really good. Maryam khanoum buys it on her way up the street where my Mom lives. The bakeries open very early.

She prefers to come early and leave early too, around 4 in the afternoon, because she lives very far away and has to change two or three buses to get home.

She cleans the apartment, prepares lunch, goes out and does some shopping for my Mom, at times, and does anything that needs to be done.

Shopping is not a problem, though. My Mom calls the local super market and gives them a list of the things she needs and they deliver her shopping at her door in no time at all. Most often my Mom goes shopping with my younger sister, who is a doctor and who habitually comes and sees her every day. They live very near one another—in the same building, but on two different floors.

As for Maryam, well she does all those things, and also comes to help when my Mom has guests. She is a very pleasant woman to have around the house. She has a very particular and young sense of humor and finds something amusing in every situation. I think it's really a blessing to be helped and served by such good natured people . . .

—ᙍ—

I went back to the bedroom and fetched some packages of fruit candy that I had brought her.

"Oh, thank you very much, are they from Paris? What nice packaging. I'll keep those for Gholamali and the children. Do you have a nice time in Paris?"

"Oh, I just work all the time and take care of my son. Yes, I enjoy teaching Business English to French businessmen and women, very nice people . . . and Charley is doing better and better in high school, so everything is all right, I guess. We miss the family, though, part of them being here, and others scattered around the world . . . you know", "but we have good friends, and that's nice".

"Khob . . ." (that means OK . . .) sometimes you can travel and visit Maman Simim",

"Khoda-ro-shokr" (meaning Thank God).

In Persian whatever happens you have to say "Thank God". This tradition and habit is based on the popular belief that if you show yourself thankful at all times, no matter what God has in store for you, and continue this attitude towards life, your perseverance will soften the heart of the Creator and will bring his favors your way. So that's all right, and you can say it abundantly, as many times as you like.

We continued to talk and have tea with toasted Barbari Bread, topped with butter, cheese and strawberry jam. A very delicious preference of mine.

I learned to make this type of 'tartine' from a good friend of mine during my university years. He used to come and have breakfast with me at my parents' before we set off for a game of tennis at the club, dressed in our tennis outfits. It is unimaginable to walk about the city in a little tennis dress "de nos jours" (in our days). I guess we had a fun and carefree youth and of course we took it for granted.

"Yes, Maryam Khanoom it's really good to be able to travel every now and then, but I wish the family were near all the time, that would have been nice. You know during the week we keep busy, and Charley's at school with his friends, but at weekends we feel like being with our family, having parties with them, receiving them, going for walks with them, and so on. You're away from your family you know what I mean."

"You know me, I work all the time," she said. "When I'm done with the work here I have my own house work to do, and I have to see to what the boys are doing, try to keep them out of mischief, and a husband, you have to take care of him too, you know".

"Bale (yes), Gholamali is a very good man—caring, responsible, hard working", added my Mom. "You've got a good guy there, Maryam, he loves you . . . and he has such a good character. You've won the good lottery."

Maryam laughed joyfully: "Yes, I know, Maman Simin".

We continued to talk about her life. She seemed to have a moment of break and I had nothing to do in particular. The persons working for you at home take their breaks any time during the morning or the afternoon. There are no set rules. They have a certain number of tasks to accomplish, and a number of hours to spend with you. They can take a tea-break whenever they feel like it. It's quite a liberal system. And with Maryam being so outspoken and natural there is absolutely no problem. My Mom enjoys her company and likes her very much.

During my holidays, on some days we would be invited to swim parties with my sister, on other days we would go shopping, or receive friends for lunch. That morning, however, there were no plans and it was too hot to go out, so we just sat there around the long oak table, covered with a fine table cloth, and we talked "de choses et d'autres". The white flowers in the crystal vase set in the middle of the table smelt really good.

My Mom took a sip of her tea and, as she was preparing a toast with cheese, she said:

"Oh, Maryam is an independent young woman, you know", "her parents, aunts and uncles live near Ramssar, not far from the 'Jadeh 2000' (the 'Road 2000'), that's where their village is, but she's been a "Tehrani" for quite a few years now, haven't you, Maryam?"

"Bale (yes), Maman Simin, that's right." "I came to Tehran when I got married. Gholamali didn't want to live in our home village; I didn't want to live in the village, either."

"But you have a beautiful village, you have the mountains and the forests nearby, and the sea is not very far, and there are such kind people in Shomal."

"I know, but we wanted to live in Tehran, there was no work in our village, just the work in the fields, I would have to work for my father like my brothers and sisters. We wanted to do something different. Gholamali had his training course in Tehran, then he was so good that the boss decided to hire him right away, it must have been because of his good character," and she laughed again.

"She prefers the big city and the pollution to the clean air of her village", said my Mom.

"The air is not so bad in Karadj, there's lots of space, there're lots of gardens." And when we lived here, when we were first married, it was nice; Niavaran is on the slopes of the mountains. The air is rather cool. There was not much pollution, we were on the garden in the studio, and we had a pink kitchen, ha, ha, ha."

"Well it was a temporary arrangement, you were newly married, you were taking care of my daughter's children and Gholamali worked nearby, it was practical for a while. It was different when the twins came."

"Bale Khanoum I agree with you, may God keep Mammad Agha ('Monsieur Mohammad). He helped us buy an apartment in Karadj." Did Zohreh Khanoum (that's me) buy a house in France for Charley?"

"No, Maryam Khanoum, I sold the one I had in the beginning, but haven't been able to buy again, yet. It's very expensive in France."

"So you don't regret having left the beautiful Shomal?" I added.

"It's Paradise where she comes from. Right on the 'Jadeh 2000'. That's the loveliest part of the country. Have you been there, Zohreh?"

"Yes, Maman, we went there with Mohammad and the three boys last year, when we went to the sea side." "The road traverses a huge open plain with villages and rice fields on both sides, and then cuts right into the forest and the mountains. It's so beautiful. We made a barbecue in the beginning of the woods on the river bank"

"Well, her village is off that road, before the mountains start."

"I worked in those fields until I was 16; it's a lot of hard work, especially for women . . . I have all my cousins, aunts and uncles there. It was good for the family gatherings and the weddings. We go and visit sometimes and also when there is a wedding in the family. Then everyone pays a lot of money to help the newly wed. It's very bad for my pocket every time." She laughed heartily at the idea.

"Oh, you have to give money instead of gifts?" I asked.

"Yes, we have to give money *and* gifts. Well they have to start a new life. Everyone helps out. The close relatives also offer jewelry and gold. It's a once-in-a-life-time thing, but I have so many cousins . . ."

"Did you get married in your village too?"

"Yes, with Gholamali. My father liked him very much."

"I wanted my cousin, but my father would not give him my hand. He said he was lazy. He came many times to ask, but my father would not agree. He had things, you know. He had a small house and some land, but he did not work very much. I think he counted on me to do that for him," and she laughed again. "Anyway, when Gholamali came, my father said yes. He is younger than me, a few years. He has kind eyes, Zohreh Khanoom, have you seen his eyes?"

"Shomali girls marry younger men." Commented my Mom. "They say it is better if the girl is older, she can then organise a man's life better. I think they've got a good point there . . ."

"So Gholamali is younger than you?"

"Bale, and he's very happy". My father said: "He is a sincere man, he has a profession and he is hard-working", and for a long time he wanted me. He waited a long time. He was very patient, he is always very patient. He lets me manage. I'm the boss" . . . and laughter . . .

"And do you manage well?"

"Yes, we get by all right, 'Khoda-ro-Shokr'. We pay for the apartment. Gholamali has a good salary. I have a budget for the household, the food and other things. I put aside some money for clothing and the trips to our village. I also try to save for a rainy day. You never know what happens. I tell Hamid to save some of his income, too. It's a good habit to have, you know."

"Yes, of course, if your expenses allow it, why not . . ." "Anyway, you manage better than I do . . ."

"Shall I bring you another tea?"

"Yes, please, that would be really nice . . ."

At this moment the door opened and my younger sister, Khandan, entered. With her, the atmosphere changes immediately and it becomes very lively. She is a busy doctor always between two appointments, coming from her hospital, going to her laboratory, going to accompany someone for an exam, going to receive a particular patient at home, or going to collect her shopping at the supermarket down the street. Usually she doesn't even take off her cotton scarf and her overall. She sits down all dressed up for a while and then she runs along to her next appointment.

Hi, '*Bonjours*'. She seemed surprised as she kissed everyone.

"Still having breakfast, at this time of the day?" "Please bring me a cup of tea Maryam jan (dear)".

It was only 10 O'clock, and I was on vacation, so I felt fine sitting there in my summer pajamas.

"Here's the program for tomorrow", she said all in one breath, "We're going to visit the Golestan Palaces and have lunch in a traditional restaurant in the 'Bazaar'. I have taken my day off to do some tourism with you guys. The girls are coming and so are Navabeh and her two sons. We're all going to meet at their home, take a cab to the new metro station at 'Mirdamad'. It's only a few stations and the new metro is really good. The stations are very artistically decorated, and it's cool in there. You must see that. It will take us a long time by car; the traffic jams are terrible in the morning *and* in the afternoon . . ." "How does that sound to you, are we all set?"

"Sounds wonderful, it's going to be lots of fun with that 'equipe' and all the young members." I said to her with good humor.

"I gotta go now, my colleagues have all taken their afternoons off, see you in the evening . . ."

I blew her a kiss and we waved Good Bye to her, as she was rushing out of the door.

"I don't know how she does it, being so active in this heat?"

"Next year I will come in the springtime", I thought to myself . . .

—✺—

"All right everyone, I'm gonna get dressed and go to Tadjrish for a walk, look at some galleries and things . . .". "Or should I go to the terrace and get tanned a little."

"No, azizam (my dear) the sun is too hot you'll get sun stoke", reflected my Mom. We all moved along.

"'Kheyly Khoob'(very good) Maryam jan, you can prepare us some 'kabab' and white rice, for lunch, and we let you organize yourself with the house and don't forget to water the plants, you should also go and get some fruit and soft drinks for my grand children". O.K? let's see, what time are my guests coming this evening?"

Florence Zohreh Zaré (FloZa) August 2004

The Driving License

I had just arrived in Tehran and I was to stay only for a few weeks. My driving license had expired a few months before and I had decided to have it extended or renewed during my stay.

—m—

It is extremely difficult to get by without a car in Tehran. You have to depend on taxies, and "agences". These are more modern, more expensive and fancier cars. As a rule you stand by the side of the street or the avenue and hold out your hand and wave to the white taxies that are going your way. They usually have their own itineraries and cover a certain distance. Some will take you from Nakhjavan to Meydan-e-Tajrish (Tajrish Square). They cover a round trip and will not go anywhere else. Some will take you from Meydan-e-Tajrish to Park Mellat, then others will take you from Park Mellat to Meydan-e-Vanak, and so on. They usually take three people on the back seat and one or two on the front seat.

It is not so bad! No matter where you are, there are always taxies that will take you to your destination, or at least somewhere close to it. They are similar to—private buses. You pay 50 Toumans or 100 Toumans (Toman=10 Rials, the Iranian currency) for each trip, depending on the distance. You can also ask such taxies, when, and if you catch one totally free, to take no other passenger and be your own private taxi all the way to your destination. Then you will have to multiply the fare by 24, or more.

The driver will most likely talk with you all along the trip and tell you all about his views on life, world affairs and what should be done, and eventually about his family life and difficulties. It is quite a challenge, because you are expected to react correctly to his arguments and discuss all these matters with him thoroughly, respond with adequate comments and advance some possible solutions to the problems enumerated. I must confess, on certain days conducting such conversational gymnastics is just beyond my power. While traveling in Tehran during those hot summer days, if I am not driving, I am usually daydreaming, or I am somewhere deep in my own thoughts, and trying very hard not to faint as the waves of hot air blow onto my face from all the open windows . . . Yes, helas the public cabs provide no air conditioning . . .

—∞—

Indeed public transport is varied and colorful in Tehran. There are also neat and modern buses which cover long long distances. A number of seats are reserved for women and a number of them are reserved for men! (As time goes by, however, this rule is less and less reinforced. Some tired men sometimes pass the barrier and take a seat in the women's section—and some women also step right ahead and take a seat in the men's section—some signs of modernity settling by itself) . . .

There is also a network of mini-buses where everybody sits together. It is difficult to understand why cabs and minibuses are unisex and buses are not. It is no doubt just another one of the numerous paradoxes that one meets in the Iranian Republic. The buses follow the same rules as the European buses. They stop only at the bus stops; whereas the mini-buses run as the cabs do, and stop wherever you ask them to stop.

At any time of the day or night, no matter where you find yourself, be it in the center of town or in the outskirts of the city, you can always find a ride home.

You feel much more independent, however, if you drive your own car, with the air-conditioning turned on to the maximum to protect you from the unbearable heat, and your favorite music to keep you company during the frequent and gigantic traffic jams in the city.

—∞—

So coming back to my driving license I felt it was necessary to have it renewed. One very hot day, as I was walking near Tajrish Square, I thought to myself: "I'll ask the men in uniform who manage the traffic. They should know what is to be done". So I looked around and saw a little octagonal brick building in the middle of the lawn that is on the northern side of the Tajrish Square. It is an annex of the National Rahnamai-va-Ranandeghi (The Traffic Guidance Bureau).

—◠◡◠—

The immense Alborz Mountains, appearing in shades of light purple in the heat of the summer day, covered half of the bright blue horizon. Tajrich Square with the large green in the center and the tall pine trees all around it stood there before the mountains. The cars were turning round and round the square, some honking their horns to the pedestrians who were trying to cross the busy square in all directions.

Tajrish in the extreme north of Tehran is quite a crowded and noisy village. A large avenue running on a few blocks, links one large square, Meydan-e-Ghods, to another large square, Meydan-e-Tajrish. The entire village is totally commercial, with different kinds of shops, selling clothes, jewelry, and food. There are also banks, cinemas, and restaurants. The great number of shoppers, visitors and passersby, make it difficult to walk quickly on the large sidewalks. So one finally has to slow down and adapt to the rather relaxed pace at which everyone walks. It is a different way of life. Not to worry and take things as they come.

Here a woman is looking for a shoe shop for her little daughter; there you can have an ice cream in an elegant pastry shop; over there is there's a shop that sells a thousand sort of spices; ten steps ahead there is a fruit shop. A little further away you come across a modern "Mall" with many entrances. The "Mall" also enters right into the middle of the Tajrish Bazaar. It is crazy, intriguing, and quite interesting to walk about these shops and the little side-streets . . . there are always some unexpected sights and interesting surprises in store for us . . .

—◠◡◠—

I tried to walk on the crossing and go to the other side of the Square. Now, crossing the streets in Tehran is a real challenge. You should think about nothing else and really concentrate and calculate the distances between you and the cars that keep on passing fast, as if you were not there at all. But you know you are on a crossing and it is your right to walk to the other side, so you take your courage by the two hands and you make an attempt on tiptoes. At that particular moment you understand perfectly well how the brave bullfighter feels while facing the bull that is coming running towards him. It is a challenge but you finally cross and regain your smile for the rest of the journey. Once you have accomplished crossing the street in Tehran without losing your temper, your courage, and your hopes, you know you can get by in any situation in Iran.

———

I walked toward the Traffic Bureau. As I was entering the parking lot of the office, and before reaching the lawn and the few steps that led the way to the office, I came across a policeman on a motorcycle. A very nice looking guy, tall and handsome, in a white shirt and navy blue trousers. He seemed to be in a pretty good mood as he was whistling a popular tune.

I thought to myself: "He looks very sure of himself and qualified, why don't I ask him?" So I approached, and as he was fixing a package on the back of his impressive motorcycle, I started talking to him: "Good morning officer . . . I'm sorry but my driving license has expired. Could you tell me what I should do to have it extended, or to get it renewed?" He looked at me through his sun glasses and said good-humoredly: "Yes, you should go to the office of Rahnamaye-va-Ranandeghi in Boulevard Saba . . . I stopped him to get my large calendar from my big, brown suede handbag, thinking that he had an interesting mustache, and saying to him:" Please let me write this down, because I may forget." Then I started to jot down the address. He was now getting settled on his motorcycle, looking at me casually through his Ray-Ban sun glasses.

———

People look at you naturally in Iran. It is not considered as bad manners or anything like that. You can also look at them moderately in interesting situations . . . It only means that you are paying attention and that you care about what they're saying to you and so on . . .

———

Coming back to our still-young-but-mature-looking officer in his white shirt and navy blue trousers, white helmet, and modern equipment, ready to take off. "Here, give me your notebook and pen, I'll write it down for you . . . so that you can have it in my handwriting . . ." (ke dast khatamo ham dashteh basheed) he said, and he smiled. Then with a lot of care he wrote in my notebook and handed it back to me together with my phosphorescent light green pen.

"Thank you so much", I said, smiling back to him. While I was trying to read his rather neat handwriting, he made a U-turn, made his motorcycle roar a little, and rode off into the street. I read aloud to myself what he had written on my notebook:

"Boulevard Saba, Jordan Boulevard, Rahnamae-va-Ranandeghi,
District One, Telephone no. 2056163, 2026464
4 Identity photos
Original Identity Card
Original Driving License
Eye Exam Form
Possibly a fine to pay for the few months' delay . . ."

Well that made my day and I thought: "Good I'm going to call these numbers and ask them what else I need to bring." Then I walked towards home. I had to stop at a fruit shop on the way and buy some fruit for my Mom.

The next day I got up earlier than usual and tried to call the numbers the officer had given me the day before. The numbers were busy. I dialed the three numbers one after the other several times, but it was useless. They were occupied, occupied.

"Maybe I should go to that address one day early in the morning . . ."

It was so hot, and being on holiday I was invited most of the time for lunch and dinner at friends' and relatives' houses. So basically I just let myself be, and followed the "crowd" of my family. Not being able to drive I went out as little as possible. It was fun being there in my mother's lovely and comfortable home; reading; listening to music; watching the news on CNN and BBC, also following some cultural and historical programs on the numerous local channels; talking with friends on the phone; getting all dressed up and going to parties.

Indeed after a year of intense activity in Paris, it was quite a luxurious pleasure to go to these gatherings, talk, and laugh and dance as our hearts desired.

—⚡—

Finding one's roots every so often is quite a pleasant feeling, and as far as I am concerned it generates positive energy. I am not a journalist in any way. I am only a dreamer, an artist *and* an eternal optimist . . .

Every time I go to Iran I float around (in the heat of the summer) and let myself be attracted by such and such an event, or travel to places that I remember from my childhood. Since people are mostly very patient and courteous, these activities each turn out to be memorable, and I always come back to my work and activities filled with such good resolutions as:

- "I'm not going to drink too much coffee anymore",
- "I'm going to take life pleasantly and with philosophy",
- "I'm not going to worry myself to death about such and such a matter",
- "I'm going to be relaxed",
- "I'm going to devote much more time to my friends and loved ones",
- "I'm not going to lose my temper over trivial matters",
- "I'm going to care more for people, instead of concentrating on my own worries and difficulties all the time"

. . . and so on, and so forth.

—⚡—

A few more days passed in the same manner, and I had not been able to contact the "Rahnamye-va-Ranadeghi" at Boulevard Saba.

Another nice sunny day, as the afternoon was gradually falling into the cool of the evening, I was walking in Meydan Tajrish (again).

—w—

We always go to Meydan Tajrish, as it is the center of the village near our house. You can find whatever you need there. Also it is a nice walk downhill and uphill. I just love to see those crowds, consisting mostly of young people, who are so varied and lively. Children are always fun and amusing, young girls and boys in the latest local fashion, older people walking calmly and discussing things.

—w—

In this early evening, as the heat of the day was turning into a pleasantly bearable warmth, and the bright turquoise blue of the sky was changing into a petroleum blue, at a moment when according to a French saying "all the cats are gray", I was passing by a group of young officers. They looked as If they were of high rank.

Although my father was military, and had reached the rank of Colonel in the late Shah's Army I do not know much about the ranks and grades in the Armed Forces.

These young officers in any case were moving together. They were a group of six or seven. They had light khaki-green shirts and khaki trousers, wore some decorations and the normal hats. They looked very calm and serious. I turned around on my steps and walked in their direction. One of them looked more important and slightly older. He walked in the middle, and the others walked around him with an attitude of respect.

So I stopped near him and said: "Good evening officer, may I ask you a question?" He listened to me calmly and—with the kind timidity that certain Moslem men have while talking to a woman—he said:

"Yes, certainly how can I help you?" "Well, you see my driving license has expired and I would like to know what I should do to have it renewed. Do I have to go to Boulevard Saba in Jordan Freeway?" I explained.

"No, not at all", he said. "If you are in the neighborhood you can ask at the Electronic Office of the Rahnamei-va-Ranandeghi Shemiranat, and that is in Shariati Avenue . . . It in a small street right next to the Bank Mellat. There's a large sign, you can't miss it. It's open from 8 to 14—and they'll give you the forms to fill to have it rapidly".

He adjusted his officer's hat on his discretely graying hair. I said:

"Thank you very much" and continued towards home.

I was delighted at the thought of not having to go to the far away offices in Boulevard Saba. I was happy to have had such kind information—from someone who obviously knew his subject well—and walked along the shops towards Nakhjavan. There I crossed the avenue to the north, stood in line for a few minutes for collective cab, then rode uphill, with my fellow cab-riders.

—⁂—

Early next morning I walked to the Electronic Office of the Rahnamei-va Ranandeghi Shemiranat, which was only a ten minutes' walk downhill. In Tehran if you want to get anything done you have to wake up at dawn and set off for gold. A small block down Shariati, there it was a branch of the Mellat Bank and a big sign of the Bureau that the officer had described to me. "So far so good".

I went up the stairs to the second floor. On the walls, there were huge posters addressed to different categories of people. Driving License Request Forms, Driving License Renewal Forms, I.D. Card Application Forms, Passport Issuance Application Forms, Passport Renewal Application Forms, Application Forms For Married Women Traveling Without Their Husbands, and so on. These posters were immense and all the possible cases were included. You would have to take a pen and paper and copy the requirements concerning *you* and then go home and bring the items needed to complete your application.

"Why not furnish the applicants with A-4 size copies of these posters, so they could take one and carry it with them?" I humbly thought.

That would have dissipated the incredible crowd of people, who were trying to copy the details of the posters.

There was no time for philosophy. I tried to write down what was required for my driving license renewal, looking over my fellow applicants' shoulders. I looked in my hand bag, I had everything with me. Only I would have to go for an eye examination, as it is required every ten years for a driving license renewal in Iran. Luckily, in their list of doctors they mentioned one whose office was right across the street. I filled in my form in two copies, and stapled my pictures to them. The fee was quite reasonable and we could pay to the cashier straight away. So I made my way through the crowd in the small office leading to the cashier's desk, slipped my papers under her arm, and said, timidly:

"I am only here for a few more days and I would appreciate it if I could have my driving license renewed during this time. Thank you so very much for your kind understanding and for your help".

She looked at me with sympathy and discretely took my papers, went through them rapidly and looked up:

"Khanoum-e-aziz", meaning dear lady, your driving license is from Shiraz, we only treat licenses from the capital. You should go to the post office and make a request by correspondence. Here you go", and she handed my papers back to me.

"Oh, no! I was so happy I was reaching the end of my quest for a renewed driving license" I thought, "and here I have to go to the post office, and start all over again." "Courage!" as the French say at such moments, "it's still quite early in the morning and there's a main post office not very far from here", "I'll just walk out there quickly while I still have my synergy, and get it done with."

So I walked down the stairs of the crowded office, stepped back on the street that was now warming up, and set off for the post office.

The nearest major post office was within twenty minutes' walking distance. The shops on my way were just opening and there were very few people in the street. Some were standing in line at a bakery shop, waiting for the fresh "Nan-e-Sangak, Nan-e-Lavash and Nan-e-Barbary", all three delicious types of Iranian beard. Breakfast with hot Nan-e-Barbary accompanied with butter and honey, with excellent Darjeeling tea is definitely a part of my happy childhood souvenirs.

This post office is quite nice. It is at the corner of two large avenues. At the entrance there is a little shop where you can buy post cards, films and such items. On the left hand side there are counters. At the first counter you can buy stamps for inside the country, at the second you can buy stamps for foreign countries, and a little further away they deal with administrative affairs. Postal services are good and efficient in Iran, very much like European postal services. The employees are for the most part courteous and helpful. Of course you have to stand in line and wait for your turn.

There were not many people queuing up at the desk where I was going—what is more all the information I wanted to have was posted on a bulletin board. It was all explained on several pages. I had to get some documents together—mostly what the motorcycle officer had told me and written in my book. I also had to get an eye exam form filled in by a designated doctor at Boulevard Saba. So I had to go to the famous Boulevard Saba after all. Quite an expedition was waiting for me.

"Let me see . . . I have to get photocopies of my driving license", "but wait a minute the date on this document is 25/3/1375 (the Iranian year), that's somewhere in June 1996 and it is valid for ten years. We are in 2004 . . .

"Oh, cool! My driving license is not expired yet. It is still valid. I don't have to go through all this just yet, it can wait another two years".

A feeling of total relief came over me and replaced the restless anguish and obsession that had invaded me during those days.

"There's nothing to hurry about", and I stepped out of that post office filled with a delicious feeling of freedom . . .

Florence Zaré (FloZa), August 2004

The Gate of Heaven

I usually enjoy traveling by plane. As the airplane was flying up into the clouds, however, I had a strong feeling of sadness and a strange thought. What if we just went up and up into the skies? What if we went up, ever ascending, never descending? The inside of the aircraft was very illuminated with the bright light coming in from the windows.

I felt lighter and lighter. Yes, what if we never descended. Way up above the clouds, we should be closer to God! Wouldn't it be a fantastic feeling to go up and up and disappear into the bright light that was sky blue at first, and then gradually turned into white?

If we go to Heaven in this brand new Airbus, we won't have to worry about our taxes that are coming in September; we won't have to worry about the bills to pay, and the debts to honor. Wow, what a lovely, relaxing, but strange thought. If we could just not go down, not hit the ground and therefore, not suffer a tragic crash onto the Earth. If we could be aspired by a cool Heavenly force into the skies and land at the Gate of Heaven!

—⚜—

Traveling by air can be a real pleasure. I think about my destination and my loved ones to see. It's only a five hour flight from Paris to Tehran, if there is no stop-over, yet each time I get very excited about it. I enjoy taking my time doing things, especially when it comes to doing the things that I like. Traveling is one of them and packing goes along with it. So I had packed my luggage and I was all set to leave for my summer holidays.

Earlier that day, however, I had had a restless feeling about this flight. I couldn't bring myself to get out of bed and get ready for my trip.

My teen-age son had come home late after a good bye party organized by his school friends. I managed to wake him up and he started to pack around nine.

Our flight was early in the afternoon and our taxi was on time. Yet, I was feeling very tense. I forgot to bring along my check book. The bank would not let me have the sum that I wanted to withdraw—"new regulations". I would have to go to the branch where my account is, but there was no time to do that. My account is in the neighboring town of Beauchamp, and if we went there we would miss our flight. I took the money that was allowed me in the nearby branch, and just said: "Thank you that will do", and rushed back to our taxi.

On the freeway there was a lot of traffic and our taxi driver—although a nice looking chap of a certain age, cool and relaxed, wearing a pair of Ray-Ban sunglasses, with his hair in large blond curls, not cut short enough, and a beard of the same nature—had taken the long way. He was reassuring us that there would be less traffic going this way.

". . . Well normally there is . . ." He mumbled as we were moving slowly in the long traffic jam. So instead of going through "Porte Maillot, Porte Dauphine, Porte d'Auteuil . . ." we had to go through "Porte de la Chapelle", "Porte de Lilas", "Porte d'Ivry" . . . and a good number of other "Portes" (Gates) of Paris to escape the metropolitan traffic, and "rouller" towards Orly Airport.

Once in Orly-Sud, we hurried to the check-in desk—which had incidentally been moved to the airport basement for a number of flights—only to find out that our departure time, originally fixed at two thirty, had been delayed to four thirty.

"The plane is flying via Cologne, you see . . ." No, we didn't quite see the reason, nor the connection, but we had no alternative than to be understanding about the last minute delay.

Then of course my young companion, my own beloved son, blamed me for having dragged him out of bed so early.

Well, as far as I'm concerned when you have plane to catch, a six hour flight the next day, you just go to bed early and try to have a good night's sleep. That would make of you a good humored travel-companion.

Now, as the French say "go and say that to a 19-year-old" who has a million things on his mind, and whose sweetheart has just left on a two-week training course to Spain. "OK, we'll have to deal with that one too".

Earlier that morning he had told me:

"I don't understand why you're always so anxious and worried, it is as if you were going to miss something important if you didn't run, run, run all the time", "Why don't you ever relax . . ." Then he added:" I think you should see a shrink . . ."! "Cerise sur le gateau" (cherry on the cake) that's just the comment I needed!

"Well, my dear young man, when I was young, there was Daddy to solve all the problems, and there weren't that many to solve. We didn't' have to worry about a thing!" "Everything was always kindly arranged by a team of helping people. All we had to do was just to be there and go places. There were never any unexpected events, never any unpleasant surprises to have to deal with. I didn't have to think, and act, 24 hours a day on all sorts of possible and impossible troubles concerning our lives. Do you think I enjoy being worried all the time?"

"Anyway let's get on with this trip. I don't quite feel this flight. I don't feel like I'm going to travel at all! I don't know the reason for this lack of motivation". Then I thought to myself:

"If I were superstitious I would feel a premonition about this flight . . . , I would say:"

"I shouldn't take it", "We should cancel it", "It feels like we're going nowhere" . . . but of course I didn't say that out aloud.

I always try to encourage myself, present a smiling face to the world. "Smile and the world will smile at you", always says my elder sister. I never intended to be "mother courage". It just happened that way . . . there's always some problem to be solved some decision to be made. It's pretty tough to be Mommy, Daddy, and the entire Family, all at the same time. This is because we live far from most of our family members, practically all year round. I try to keep busy and I am busy most of the time, so there's no time to be sad. It's a technique to develop. Never to be sad, zooming through Monday to Friday as if in some kind of a "fast forward motion", always looking forward to something nice, having selective memory, just remembering the good parts, and disregarding the hectic parts . . . with: "le passé est passé, vive le future" as motto . . .

—◠◠—

Despite all the good will in the world and my depression-escaping practices, I felt really down-hearted in the airport cafeteria where we were having lunch, my son and I.

I showed him this really lovely place in the airport, a special cafeteria that not many people know about. This was in view of having a relaxed lunch and starting our holidays peacefully and in good humor. I wanted to be seated towards the interior, where the tables were nice and cozy, and where we could see the other people. They looked like an interesting bunch. With my son insisting, however, we ended up sitting right next to the huge front window, where we could see all the airplanes and none of the people in the restaurant. The light was so bright it was hurting my eyes. I felt like a butterfly sticking to the huge window!

I was so upset that tears started filling my eyes. "I'll go to the ladies' room for a minute", I said, as I was getting up and turning my head the other way so that he couldn't see my tears.

I am very sensitive by nature, and as we say in Persian "I have my tears in my sleeves" . . .

So I left my son to his thoughts for a little while. When, having wiped away my tears, I came back to our table; I realized a kind looking guy had settled at the small round table next to ours. He could be German for all I know. A German guy in his fifties . . . with a smile in his eyes . . . white hair . . . busy reading his news paper.

—⚒—

The plane was going up and up over the white cotton clouds. I closed my eyes and imagined us arriving at the large and magnificent Gate of Heaven. We were just gliding, gliding and coming to a stop slowly.

There, right next to the Gate was standing a very tall and nice-looking guy, with navy blue eyes and a very kind smile. Oh it was my very first love, my modern time Viking.

We had had a romance one summer across the USA and all across the Atlantic Ocean. That was followed by a four-year correspondence that I had kept dearly until just before my marriage. I could nearly hear his good natured laughter. Because of the divine feeling I had shared with him those years—I had wanted to be incinerated when I died, and my ashes to be blown over the Atlantic Ocean . . . I would never ever forget him. It was all so innocent and adorable.

He was wearing a long white robe, as one would, standing there next to the Gate of Heaven, holding the Gate open for someone quite special, me that is.

Further to the right I could see my boyfriend from my university years, looking nice and tanned, standing there as if waiting for something, and looking kind of worried.

I remember those days. I used to wear black a T-shirt and jeans most of the time. He had a happy-go-lucky attitude and a "predator's smile". Underneath the easy going appearances, though, he had very deep mystical feelings. Seeing him waiting there reminded me of the two years we had spent together, and the at-times-stormy relationship that we had had, and of course, his warm embrace.

Closer to me on the left hand side I could see the thoughtful profile of my first husband. I had spent 15 years of my life with him. No wonder he was closer. He appeared to be preoccupied by his own thoughts, looking as unpredictable as in real life, with his grey-green eyes, searching his own horizons . . .

Still closer on the left I could see another gentleman friend of mine, standing there. His hair was rather long and carefree. He was looking at me with his kind dark eyes. Why was he sad? We lost him several years ago when he had a heart attack. He was a wonderful young man and certainly should have lived a long and happy life. He had been so kind to me. Only good memories . . .

—⚏—

I was deeply absorbed by my dreamy thoughts and my imagination. It was quite a romantic picture to contemplate. The golden Gate of Heaven, shining through the white clouds, with all the guys I had loved standing here and there. They were all transmitting their good vibrations of caring and attention for me, as if wanting to make me feel welcome to the Gate. It felt quite good to feel loved and cared for. I guess I had a need for that heavenly feeling right at that moment.

There were other forms and shapes, other faces scattered in the clouds, but of less importance and I didn't want to think about them. I just wanted to feel the presence of those whom I had really cared for. It was a nice enveloping feeling.

—ᴡ—

We were still in the plane. The sky outside had turned to dark blue. We seemed to be moving along smoothly. It was like being carried by a huge white feather, blown by the mid-summer breeze . . . on top of the cotton clouds. I felt incredibly light.

—ᴡ—

My son was absorbed in his book, looking very serious and distant. Maybe he was thinking about his girlfriend. "What would she be doing in Spain right now"? I don't know. Teen-age life has its own mysteries.

We have a wonderful relationship, my son and I. Normally we get along exceptionally well. We are very close to one another and we talk about many subjects together.

I never let him go to school without a well-balanced breakfast of orange juice and vitamins, serials, "tartines" and a glass of milk. Every evening I set a lovely table and we have dinner together and talk about all kinds of subjects. We sometimes eat out, go to the movies, to the galleries. We have a pretty good relationship. I make sure he studies well and he is well organized for school. I make sure he lacks nothing. He's rather reasonable and does not go out a lot, just the weekends.

He usually spends all his holidays with his cousins and our family all around the world. He has a kind, warm and caring character, and he's quite intelligent. We stay good friends most of the time. I respect his private garden, though. That's when he is deep in his own thoughts, the mysteries of growing up . . . I always respect people's private gardens. Sometimes there's a sign, "No Entrance". That's fine. I never dig into such situations. It's one of the rules of my "don't touch the ground" policy. It helps me carry on . . . helps me keep the balance . . .

We had had two meals already. "They feed you very well on this airline", I thought. "That keeps you busy until landing time".

I still can't believe how a huge thing like an Airbus can stay up in the air for so long. That is probably why everybody applauds, and there are cries of joy and relief when the plane finally lands. It's always wonderful to come back to Earth and touch the ground gracefully. It makes us remember, we're the lucky inhabitants of this Planet.

So let's get our hand luggage and follow the crowd to the exit, walk down the steps into the hot dry air of Iran. After the passport control and the formalities we get to see our family. My brother and sister, their children, and sometimes my mom, come to meet us at the airport. And it's really quite lovely to see them each time. As William Shakespeare said so beautifully: "Parting is such sweet sorrow" and as I always humbly think: "Getting together is such heart-warming joy . . ."

Yes, we need these trips "pour recharger nos batteries", to recharge our emotional and affectionate batteries and to be ready again for our busy Parisian lives . . .

Florence Zohreh Zaré (FloZa) August, 2006

I AM A PEARL,
I AM AN ISLAND

I am a Pearl, I am an Island

My history goes back to about 3000 years ago. Throughout the centuries I have been given different names, Kamtina, Arakia, Arakata, Ghiss, and Kish in more recent times.

Where to Find Me

Located in the light green waters of the Persian Gulf, close to the southern coastline of the Iranian Mainland, I am a small coral island with palm trees scattered along my white sandy shores. If you swim in my light green, crystal clear waters you will meet colonies of colorful fish that swim with you trustfully, and if you dive more deeply you will have a more spectacular sight of the coral edged lagoons and the marvelous sea life.

My surface is not very large, only 90 square kilometers and my shape is oval. My land is mostly flat and sandy, with the highest point of only 45 meters above sea level.

My Climate

The air that I breathe can be temperate and pleasant from November to March. You can come then, and share the refreshing natural beauty and casual lifestyle that I offer to my visitors.

During the summer, however, you would not want to visit. The hot humid breeze that caresses my sand would be unbearable to your fragile human skins. You can come of course and spend most of your time in the huge, air conditioned, shopping centers and luxury hotels that have been built for your pleasure.

My Sea Life

My sheltered waters of coral-edged lagoons are home to many of the world's spices of reef fish. If you go snorkeling or scuba diving you will have a spectacular view of sea life beneath my waters. I am often called the pearl of the Persian Gulf, for I am a heaven of peace and tranquility fringed by sandy shores and coral reefs. I am home of friendly colorful fish that I watch over with care.

My Pearls

I have always been known for the quality of my pearls. Historians have written that while the famous traveler Marco Polo was visiting the court of Imperial China he was fascinated by the beauty of the pearls worn by the Emperor's wives. He was told that they had come from my shores.

My Nationality

Naturally I am Persian. My beauty, however, has attracted different Nations, since immemorial times.

My Fortune

In the 14th century, during the reign of Hormoz, I fell into an unfortunate decline. My destiny remained obscure until recent times. During the reign of the late Shah of Iran I became a private retreat for the guests of the Nation. With my own international airport, palaces, luxury hotels and restaurants I became an ideal holiday resort.

Shortly after the Iranian Revolution I began to be treated differently. I was then given the status of a free zone. A team of managers were designated to work on my development. Since some very good facilities were already in place, their task was carried out smoothly and well.

My Recent Development

I have been developing remarkably well over the recent years. My eastern coast has been changed into a vast building site, resembling more and more an attractive holiday resort. Many people have been investing on my lands. I now carry more than 15 tourist lodgings complexes, beautiful villas, guesthouses and hotels. I have all a modern town can desire; power and water supplies, advanced telecommunications systems, and very modern transportation facilities.

As you land on my surface and travel from one side to the other you will notice the abundance of brand new, latest-model comfortable, white cars that serve as cabs. For all these reasons I am sure to have a prosperous and promising future. I find that flattering and of course it makes me very happy.

At times I feel pretty independent. I have my own flag, for instance. There are signs in English everywhere, as English it the international language that most of my visiting tourists speak and understand.

Most likely in the future there will be an even greater influx of tourists and visitors towards my shores. People say that I am different from the mainland of Iran, and that once you are here life becomes a permanent party and an enjoyable holiday.

What I Offer to My Visitors

On my lovely seashores you will find men-only and women—only beaches. Well, I live under the Islamic law these days. You can also go boating, cycling, diving, fishing, jogging, and have a cheerful and unforgettable stay. Usually when you leave you promise to come back again.

In addition to my sandy coral beaches, I have an Aquarium where a variety of colorful fish have been gathered to show you the fascinating picture of the underwater world in the warm waters of the Persian Gulf.

Another attractive place to visit is the "Pearl Culturing and Developing Center". You can also choose to have a flight in a helicopter and contemplate the shiny light green waters of the Persian Gulf.

Or, you can visit the ancient ruins of the historical city of "Harireh" that remain on my surface from some 800 years ago. I still remember that city. The famous Persian poet Saa'di mentioned it in his book of poems "Golestan".

Another option is to discover the traditional Persian music by attending one of the many concerts that are held in my theatres all year round. And if you enjoy singing, you can have meals in some of my luxury restaurants and sing along with the popular singers who entertain my guests.

Before You Leave

You will realize that your holidays have passed by very fast and you will want them to start all over again.

If you take off one evening on a jet plane and fly back to the Iranian Mainland, make sure you wave good-bye to me, and look at my calm, white coral surface as you gain altitude. Remember my neatly traced roads, lit along the night and promise to come back soon for another visit.

Florence Zohreh Zaré, (FloZa), February 2007

Source for historical data : The local press of the Island of Kish